The Marvelous McCrittersons™

ROAD TRIP TO GRANDMA'S

Stan ★ Margie ★ Frank ★ Alice ★ Auggie

Art by
Greg Paprocki

★

Words by
Beth Paprocki

DOVER PUBLICATIONS, INC.
Mineola, New York

D0897400

Copyright

Copyright © 2015 by Greg Paprocki, Inc.
All rights reserved.

Bibliographical Note

The Marvelous McCrittersons: Road Trip to Grandma's is a
new work, first published by Dover Publications, Inc., in 2015.

International Standard Book Number

ISBN-13: 978-0-486-79383-2
ISBN-10: 0-486-79383-4

Manufactured in the United States by Courier Corporation
79383401   2015
www.doverpublications.com

Grab your crayons and join the McCrittersons—a family of five cheerful raccoons—as they go on a long drive to visit Grandma and Grandpa. Every page is full of excitement, from packing bags and driving on the highway, to truck stops and roadside attractions. And when they finally arrive at Grandma and Grandpa's, it's time for even more family fun!

Morning's here! Time to pack!
Tablet, books—what kind of snack?

More **toys!** More **clothes!** Water to drink.
Take everything but the kitchen **sink!**

BUZZZZZZ

Mom has cooked a **hearty meal** to keep **Dad bright** behind the wheel.

6

GRAMPY'S Oatmeal

Wheat Bread

MILK

Raisins

yummy

yeah!

The car is packed, the engine's warm!
We're on our way to Grandma's farm!

All the neighbors have come to say,
"**Have fun!** Travel **safe!** Be on your way!"

While Mom helps Dad navigate the map,
the kids are too excited to nap.

BANK

Yummy
GROCERY

Traffic's tight, better **slow down!**
But we'll stop for **lunch** in the next town.

SPEED
LIMIT
65

Yummy burgers,
   fries and a shake!
What a wonderful
way to **take a break!**

Steps and slides.
Now these
are **rides!**

A detour to a roadside attraction
gives the kids a
much-needed **DISTRACTION.**

DINO PARK

What a great big dinosaur!

Push the button,

hear him

ROAR!

PRESS

SWOOSH goes the dino swing.

Gas up at the truck stop—
we all get a **treat!**
Mom got us sunglasses
that are super **neat.**

Off of the highway, down old country roads,
passing farmers and tractors,
and crops being sowed.

The journey is over—
we're finally **here!**

Grandpa shouts out,
"They've arrived,
my **dear!**"

This day calls for a
BIG celebration!

Everyone's filled with such JOY and **elation!**

Grandpa's favorite thing to do?
Grilling **veggies** on the
barbecue!

Tucked cozy in bed, Grandma gives us a **kiss**.
We will always remember moments like **this!**